SOUPERCHICKEN

AUNT CLARISSA

AUNT EMILY

AUNT LIZ

AUNT ZOE

AUNT GOLDA

AUNT OLIVE

HENRIETTA

Mary Jane and Herm Auch

Holiday House / New York

For reading teachers everywhere

Text copyright © 2003 by Mary Jane Auch
Illustrations copyright © 2003 by Herm Auch and Mary Jane Auch
All Rights Reserved
Printed in the United States of America
www.holidayhouse.com

Library of Congress Cataloging-in-Publication Data
Auch, Mary Jane.
Souperchicken / Mary Jane and Herm Auch.—1st ed.
p. cm.
Summary: When Henrietta becomes the first chicken in her coop
to learn how to read, she uses her skills to save her aunties
from becoming chicken soup.
ISBN 0-8234-1704-2 (hardcover)
ISBN 0-8234-1829-4 (paperback)
[1. Chickens—Fiction. 2. Domestic animals—Fiction.
3. Reading—Fiction.]
I. Auch, Herm, ill. II. Title.
PZ7.A898 Sw 2003
[Fic]—dc21   2002068914

Henrietta loved to read. She started by reading names on the trucks that passed the farm. Soon she could sound out words on the feed sacks, even big ones like *hydro-yucka-fizzamine*. Then she read whole sentences in the books and newspapers the farmer left behind after his coffee breaks. Henrietta began taking her own coffee breaks, not for coffee but for the pure joy of reading.

"Henrietta, you waste so much time,"
squawked Aunt Golda.
   "She hasn't laid one egg this week,"
Aunt Zoe complained.
   Henrietta wasn't interested in laying eggs.
She'd much rather read.

Could
The sky
Fall?

By Chick N. Little

But Henrietta wasn't the only hen not laying well.

"Egg production is way down," the farmer said. "Time to send these old hens on vacation."

"I hope we're going to the beach," clucked Aunt Emily.

"I'd rather play golf," squawked Aunt Morissa.

A truck came the next day. "Let's get you ladies packed for your vacation," the farmer said.

The truck driver chuckled. "This is your chance to veg out, girls."

"You can just noodle away your time."

"Yep, just simmer down and relax."

The men laughed at their
jokes as they loaded the hens
into crates.
   Henrietta didn't see
what was so funny. That
was odd because she usually
got the jokes in the comic strips.
   The driver reached for Henrietta.

"Leave that young one here," said the farmer. "She owes me hundreds of eggs before she earns her vacation."

The driver laughed. "You think she'll rice to the occasion?"

"Sure, she's a cream of a chicken. It'll be egg drop all over the place once she gets started."

"No wonder you're wonton to keep her."

The two men went into fits of laughter again, slapping each other on the back.

"Now aren't you sorry you didn't work harder?" Aunt Emily clucked.

"You'll miss our lovely vacation," cackled Aunt Liz.

"That's what she gets for being lazy," said Aunt Golda.

Henrietta's head drooped. "I didn't mean to be lazy."

"Have a nice time, aunties," Henrietta cried. "Send postcards!" She didn't hear a cluck of good-bye.

Then the driver handed the farmer a wad of money.

"That's strange," said Henrietta. "Why would the driver pay to take my aunties on vacation?"

As the truck made a big circle in the driveway, Henrietta saw the answer.

"Souper Soup Company! I must rescue them!"

Henrietta ran headlong down the driveway, flapping her wings. "You have to escape! They're going to make you into soup!" The truck's engine drowned out her cries.

As the truck pulled onto the road, Henrietta jumped onto the back bumper.

It was hard enough hanging on as the truck rumbled
down the winding farm road, but when it sped up on
the expressway, Henrietta almost lost her grip. "I
have to be strong," she gasped. Then as the truck hit
full speed, Henrietta was blown off the bumper and
tumbled into the ditch.

When she got to her feet, Henrietta saw a supermarket.
"Just what I need."

She
"Oh, d
read t
Beakvi
the ad
get of

Henrietta waited at the toll booth and jumped on the next truck that stopped. It was filled with pigs.

"Are you going on vacation with us?" one pig asked.

"Vacation? Sounds fishy to me. I'll check it out." Henrietta read the letters on the truck.

"Saucy Sausage Company. That's a bad sign."

Henrietta told the pigs about their fate. "When
this truck stops, you must run for your lives!"
Then the truck turned at the wrong exit.
"I have to leave," Henrietta said. "Good luck. And
please learn to read so you don't get tricked again."
The pigs promised
that they would.

SAUCY SAUSAGE
COMPANY

Henrietta rolled down into the ditch, brushed herself off, and flew to an overhead sign. This time she leaped onto a truck filled with cows. "Going on vacation?" she asked.

They were.

Henrietta read the truck sign. "Happy Hamburger Company!" She warned the cows about being made into burgers. Then the truck pulled off at a rest stop. "No time to rest. Everybody run! And please learn to read! Reading can save your lives!"

Henrietta jumped onto a truck covered with a tarp. Suddenly she heard clucking. Could it be? She read the sign on the truck. "Souper Soup Company! Aunt Golda! Aunt Morissa, Aunt Emily! Are you here?"

"Nobody here by those names," a hen clucked. "Were your aunts going on vacation?"

"This is not a vacation!" Henrietta squawked, pulling back the tarp. "They're going to make you into chicken soup!"

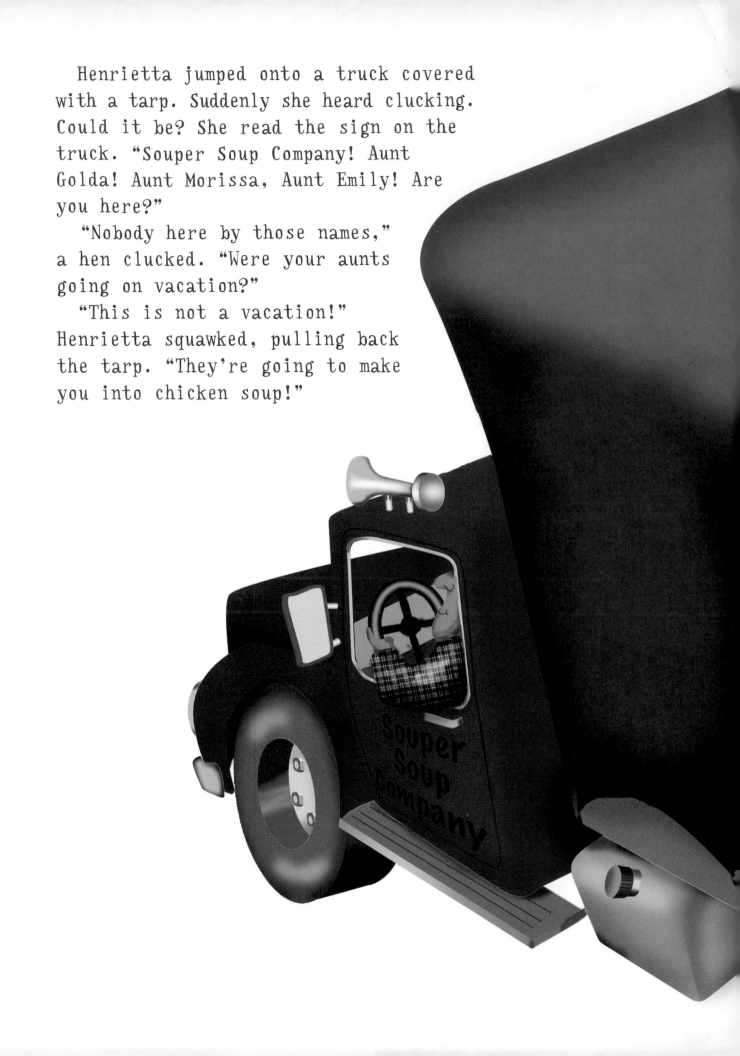

This set off such a commotion, Henrietta had a terrible time calming down the hens. By the time they arrived at the Souper Soup Company, Henrietta had everyone ready, but she was worried. "I hope my sweet aunties aren't soup yet!"

When the driver stopped the truck, the hens escaped in an explosion of squawks and feathers.

Henrietta slipped through a door and started reading the signs in the hallway. "Holding Room, Beheading Room, Plucking Room, Canning Room. Oh, dear! If they've gone beyond this first room, it's too late."

There were complicated instructions on the Holding Room door that involved pecking out the word *noodle* with her beak. The door opened!

"Aunties, it's me, Henrietta. Are you here?"

"You should have stayed home," called Aunt Golda. "This is a rotten hotel."

"There's no beach," added Aunt Emily.

"No golf course, either," said Aunt Morissa.

Remembering how upset the hens in the truck had become, Henrietta decided not to explain about the soup. "I'm opening the cages. Then you must follow close behind me and keep running until I tell you to stop."

"What are you, the activities director?" Aunt Liz squawked. "I want to rest, not run my drumsticks off."

"Me too," said Aunt Olive. "Where's my hammock?"

"Take us to a mall," said Aunt Zoe. "Let's buy what the young chicks are wearing."

"You'll be wearing a can if you don't come with me!" Henrietta screeched. "This is a chicken soup factory!"
The hens were terrified, but they followed Henrietta through the factory and out the main door.

They ran their drumsticks off until Henrietta
found a winding road with small farms tucked along
its length. Then she paused at each mailbox to check
what was inside.

"What are you looking for?"
asked Aunt Liz.
   "Clues," said Henrietta.
   "What kind of clues?" asked
Aunt Olive.

"Clues like this." Henrietta pulled out a copy of *The Versatile Vegetarian*. "We'll be safe here. This lady doesn't eat chicken."

"How do you know?" asked Aunt Emily.

"I know because I can read."

Henrietta went up to the farmhouse. The farmer was delighted to see her. She told Henrietta that she didn't eat beef but kept cows for milk. She didn't eat pork but kept pigs for digging truffles. And best of all, she didn't eat chicken, but she liked to have eggs for breakfast and an occasional quiche.

Henrietta went back to report to the others. "The farmer wants us to live here. She even has jobs for us."

"A job!" squawked Aunt Morissa. "We never got a vacation."

Henrietta smiled. "You'll like this job. We're supposed to eat the bugs in her big organic vegetable garden."

"Eating bugs isn't work," clucked Aunt Liz. "That's delicious."

From then on, Henrietta's aunties had a wonderful time patrolling the garden for bugs.

And Henrietta took on an important new career. She became a reading teacher.

The cat
sat on
the hat.

Pulling Yourself
Back Together

By Humpty Dumpty

Great
Eggsperts

By Dahls Chickens

Could
The sky
Fall?

By Chick N. Little